YO-YOS

by Cathy Hope

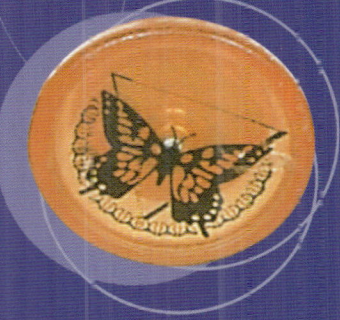

PM Nonfiction

Emerald

U.S. Edition © 2013 HMH Supplemental Publishers
10801 N. MoPac Expressway
Building #3
Austin, TX 78759
www.hmhsupplemental.com

Text © 2001 Cathy Hope
Illustrations © 2001 Cengage Learning Australia Pty Limited
Originally published in Australia by Cengage Learning Australia

15 16 17 18 19   1957   22 21 20 19 18 17 16
4500605933

Text: Cathy Hope
Photographs: photolibray.com/Hulton Getty pp. 5, 9; Pix p. 7/John D. Boyll p. 8/Genesis
Space Photo Library p.11; Bill Thomas pp titles, contents, 4, 6, 10, 12-22.

Printed in China by 1010 Printing International Ltd

Yo-yos
ISBN 978 0 76 357456 7

Contents

CHAPTER 1
History of the Yo-yo

Did you know that the yo-yo is the second-oldest known toy in the world? (The doll is the oldest known toy.)

The fun and challenge of spinning a yo-yo has been a popular activity for children and adults all over the world for thousands of years.

Crazes come and go. Sometimes yo-yos are extremely popular, then they seem to disappear. Suddenly, a new yo-yo is designed or someone invents an amazing trick, and the craze starts again.

Greece

We know from a vase in the Museum of Athens that young people in Greece played with a yo-yo-shaped object at least 2,500 years ago.

The picture on the vase *(see right)* shows a young person using a **terracotta** "disk." The disk is similar to what we now call the yo-yo.

People in Ancient Greece had ceremonies in which they offered gifts to their gods. Young people would give a favorite toy, such as a disk, to signify that they had grown up.

One of these terracotta disks is in the Museum of Athens. Dated at 500 BC, it is thought to be the oldest surviving "yo-yo."

Alaska

For many centuries, the people of Alaska have played with a toy called a "chuk-chuk," now known as the Eskimo yo-yo.

Over the years, a variety of materials have been used to make these yo-yos. Materials were used that were handy, such as fur and leather. Some yo-yos were even woven from grass.

How to use an Eskimo yo-yo

Swing one cone around in a clockwise direction. Then swing the other cone around in a counterclockwise direction. See how long you can keep both cones spinning.

Europe

Two hundred years ago, yo-yos were very popular with children and adults in Europe.

This painting shows the Duke of Normandy as a young boy, playing with a yo-yo. This picture was painted in France in 1789.

In 1791, yo-yos in Paris were called the "jou jou de Normandie." These yo-yos were mostly made from glass and ivory.

In June of 1815, the Battle of Waterloo was fought between the French and the English. Many soldiers on both sides had yo-yos to play with when they were not fighting!

Philippines

The word "yo-yo" originates from the Tagalog people of the Philippines. Yo-yo is the Filipino word for "come come," meaning come back. In 1860, the word *yo-yo* was recorded for the first time in a Filipino dictionary.

For more than one hundred years, the yo-yo has been very popular with both children and adults in the Philippines.

Some people enjoy carving their own yo-yos, and they paint or etch them with different designs, such as palm trees, birds, or the sea.

North America

In America, the yo-yo was called a *bandalore* until the 1920s when Pedro Flores, a Filipino yo-yo expert, made the toy very popular and the name "yo-yo" began to be used.

The first yo-yos manufactured in America were made out of wood. Maple, a **hardwood**, was often used. The wood needed to be air dried, then **kiln** dried before it could be made into a yo-yo. This process took at least six months.

Plastic yo-yos were first sold in the 1950s. They were much quicker and easier to make than wooden yo-yos.

Now most yo-yos are made out of plastic.

CHAPTER 2

Technology of the Yo-yo

A well-made yo-yo is a finely tuned machine that depends on **balance**, weight, and **precision** in order to perform well.

Yo-yos are also dependent on gravity. When you release a wound-up yo-yo, gravity pulls it to Earth. Gravity will hold the yo-yo down unless you provide an upward pull—by flicking your wrist to bring the yo-yo back up the string, before the spinning has stopped.

Yo-yos in Space

On April 12, 1985, NASA sent a yo-yo into space on Space Shuttle *Discovery* as part of the "Toys in Space" project.

Astronauts found that they had to use force to throw the yo-yo down to the end of its string. It couldn't just be dropped as it can be on Earth, as there was no gravity to pull the yo-yo down.

Without the downward force of gravity, the yo-yo wouldn't spin, either.

On July 31, 1992, a yo-yo was sent up on Space Shuttle *Atlantis* so that a video could be made of astronaut Jeffrey Holfman yo-yoing in slow motion. This space yo-yo traveled around the world 127 times!

CHAPTER 3
How Yo-yos Are Made

Over the years, yo-yos have been made from many different materials, including terracotta, bone, wood, glass, steel, **aluminum**, plastic, and even candy.

Making a Wooden Yo-yo

A wooden yo-yo can be made out of a single piece of wood.

1. The wood is first shaped into a cylinder on a **lathe**.

2. The cylinder is then cut down to the size of a yo-yo. Then a deep groove is cut in the center of the yo-yo to create the **axle**.

3. Each side of the yo-yo is shaped, sanded, and polished.

4. The yo-yo is taken off the lathe, and a string is wound around it. The yo-yo is now ready to use.

Making a Plastic Yo-yo

A plastic yo-yo is made up of many parts.

string   delta springs   plastic yo-yo shells
(with ball bearings)

clear caps

axle

1. A delta (with ball bearings) and a spring are placed inside a yo-yo shell. A clear or decorative cap is then firmly fixed on top, using a manual press. Each yo-yo half is assembled in this same way.

2. The axle is then screwed into one of the yo-yo halves. The winding machine winds the string onto the axle and joins the two yo-yo halves together.

3. The yo-yo is now finished and ready to be packaged.

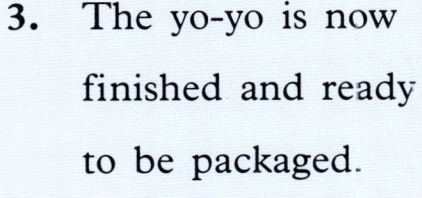

CHAPTER 4

Making Your Own Yo-yos

In the past, many yo-yos were made so that they wouldn't come apart. You'll find that most well-made modern yo-yos are now able to be taken apart. This makes it much easier to change strings. Look at a yo-yo when it has been taken apart and it will give you some clues as to how it was made.

Button Yo-yos

In the early part of the twentieth century, children in Scotland would sometimes make yo-yos out of buttons.

Button yo-yos are easy to make.

You will need two large buttons of equal size and shape, and some sewing thread.

Sew the two buttons together, then wind on a length of sewing thread to use as the yo-yo string.

Lid Yo-yos

Yo-yos can also be made from metal and plastic lids and a yo-yo string, which you can buy at a toy store.

1. Choose a pair of matching metal or plastic lids. Experiment with the lids, as you may find that they work better facing inward.

2. Plastic lids may need to be weighted to give better balance. You can do this by pressing equally sized pieces of clay onto each lid.

3. You can make the axle out of nails, knitting needles, skewers, or a wooden dowel. An adult will need to help you cut it to the right size.

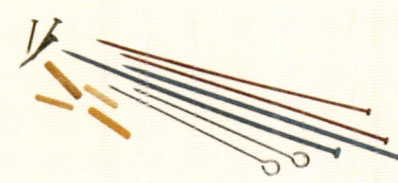

4. Mark the center of each lid, then attach the axle using strong glue.

5. Once the glue has dried, tie the yo-yo string to the axle. Your yo-yo is now ready.

CHAPTER 5

Using Your Yo-yo

You can become very skilled at using a yo-yo. The more you practice, the better you will be able to perform the tricks. Good luck!

Preparing Your Yo-yo

Before you begin to play with your yo-yo, it is important that you check the following:

1. Adjust the yo-yo string to your height

Your yo-yo shouldn't hit the floor when the string is all the way extended. If it does, it means that your yo-yo string is too long. Here's how to check if the string is the right length:

a. Let the yo-yo drop and unwind until it touches the floor.

b. With the yo-yo touching the floor, adjust the string so that it measures about 3 inches from the loop on your finger down to your waistline.

2. Correct string tension

An easy way to correct string tension is to take the string off your finger, and let the yo-yo hang straight down. The string will unwind by itself.

3. If your string is too tight

Hang the yo-yo until it unwinds completely. Then rotate it counterclockwise to make it looser.

4. If your string is too loose

Hang the yo-yo until it unwinds, then rotate it counterclockwise to make it tighter.

5. Replacing the string

Replace the string on the yo-yo when it becomes frayed, knotted, dirty, or too stiff.

The best yo-yo string is made from 100% cotton. Most suppliers of yo-yos also stock replacement strings.

Getting Started

1. Put the loop at the end of the string over your middle finger, just behind the first joint. (To stop the string flying off your finger, have the loop fairly tight.) Make sure you select a spot on your finger that feels comfortable to you.

2. Try to master the backhand throw, as it will give you plenty of spin to do tricks:

    a. With your wrist up and your arm bent, throw your yo-yo downward with a flip of your wrist.

    b. Keep your arm out straight and your hand steady as the yo-yo goes down.

    c. Give your yo-yo a slight tug up when it reaches the end of the string to return it to your hand.

Chapter 6
Yo-yo Tricks

There are well over one hundred known yo-yo tricks. A great yo-yo player named Barney Akers named most of them, such as the one called "Walk the Dog." Once you know how to control your yo-yo and have mastered some of the tricks, try inventing your own. It's fun!

The best way to learn new tricks is from other yo-yo fans. Perhaps you could also share your skills with a younger person who is anxious to learn. On the next few pages you will see some of the more popular tricks.

The Spinner

Throw your yo-yo down, and, as it reaches the bottom of the string, keep your hand still to encourage the yo-yo to spin at the end of the string. Just before the yo-yo stops spinning, give it a little tug and it will come up again.

Walk the Dog

When you have mastered "The Spinner," try "Walk the Dog."

You'll need a smooth floor or surface for this trick.

Throw a fast spinner and carefully lower the yo-yo to the ground, letting it roll along in front of you.

Around the World

You will need plenty of space for this trick.

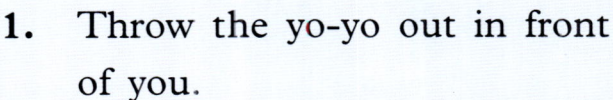

1. Throw the yo-yo out in front of you.

2. While the yo-yo is spinning at the end of the string, swing it around counterclockwise, in a big circle.

When you get good at this trick, you might be able to go "Around the World" up to ten times before the yo-yo stops spinning!

Rock the Baby

To be successful at this trick, you need to be able to spin the yo-yo at the end of the string for at least five seconds. You also need to learn to do the following moves really quickly:

1. Throw a fast spinner.

2. Wrap the middle of the string over the thumb of your other hand.

3. With your yo-yo hand, pick up the string about 3–4 inches from the yo-yo.

4. Drop your other hand down to form the base of the string triangle and swing the yo-yo back and forth.

Glossary

aluminum   a light, silvery metal that can be easily shaped

axle   a bar or center pin on which a wheel or pair of wheels spin

balance   equal weight on each side

craze   when many people want to do the same thing

hardwood   wood that is tough and lasts a long time

kiln   a furnace or oven used for baking or drying clay or wood

lathe   a machine for shaping wood; the wood spins at high speeds against a cutting tool

precision   working with accuracy

terracotta   reddish-brown baked earth or fired clay

Index